Dear Parents and Educators,

Welcome to Penguin Young Readers! As parents and educators, you know that each child develops at his or her own pace—in terms of speech, critical thinking, and, of course, reading. Penguin Young Readers recognizes this fact. As a result, each Penguin Young Readers book is assigned a traditional easy-to-read level (1–4) as well as a Guided Reading Level (A–P). Both of these systems will help you choose the right book for your child. Please refer to the back of each book for specific leveling information. Penguin Young Readers features esteemed authors and illustrators, stories about favorite characters, fascinating nonfiction, and more!

The Clubhouse

LEVEL 3

GUIDED READING LEVEL **J**

This book is perfect for a **Transitional Reader** who:
- can read multisyllable and compound words;
- can read words with prefixes and suffixes;
- is able to identify story elements (beginning, middle, end, plot, setting, characters, problem, solution); and
- can understand different points of view.

Here are some **activities** you can do during and after reading this book:
- Compound Words: A compound word is made when two words are joined together to form a new word. First look for the following compound words in the story: clubhouse, newspapers, hardware, inside. On a separate sheet of paper, write down the definition for each compound word. Next, break each word into two separate words and write down the meaning for each word.
- Instructions: In this story, the kids build a clubhouse. Pretend you are trying to explain to a friend how to build a clubhouse. Reread the story and write down the steps you would take and the materials you need to build a clubhouse.

Remember, sharing the love of reading with a child is the best gift you can give!

—Bonnie Bader, EdM
  Penguin Young Readers program

*Penguin Young Readers are leveled by independent reviewers applying the standards developed by Irene Fountas and Gay Su Pinnell in *Matching Books to Readers: Using Leveled Books in Guided Reading*, Heinemann, 1999.

Penguin Young Readers
Published by the Penguin Group
Penguin Group (USA) Inc., 375 Hudson Street, New York, New York 10014, USA
Penguin Group (Canada), 90 Eglinton Avenue East, Suite 700, Toronto, Ontario M4P 2Y3, Canada
(a division of Pearson Penguin Canada Inc.)
Penguin Books Ltd, 80 Strand, London WC2R 0RL, England
Penguin Ireland, 25 St Stephen's Green, Dublin 2, Ireland (a division of Penguin Books Ltd)
Penguin Group (Australia), 707 Collins Street, Melbourne, Victoria 3008, Australia
(a division of Pearson Australia Group Pty Ltd)
Penguin Books India Pvt Ltd, 11 Community Centre, Panchsheel Park, New Delhi—110 017, India
Penguin Group (NZ), 67 Apollo Drive, Rosedale, Auckland 0632, New Zealand
(a division of Pearson New Zealand Ltd)
Penguin Books (South Africa), Rosebank Office Park, 181 Jan Smuts Avenue,
Parktown North 2193, South Africa
Penguin China, B7 Jiaming Center, 27 East Third Ring Road North,
Chaoyang District, Beijing 100020, China

Penguin Books Ltd, Registered Offices: 80 Strand, London WC2R 0RL, England

Copyright © 2002 by Ezra Jack Keats Foundation. All rights reserved. Text by Anastasia Suen.
Illustrations by Allan Eitzen. First published in 2002 by Viking and in 2003 by Puffin Books, imprints of
Penguin Group (USA) Inc. Published in 2013 by Penguin Young Readers, an imprint of Penguin Group
(USA) Inc., 345 Hudson Street, New York, New York 10014. Manufactured in China.

The Library of Congress has cataloged the Viking edition
under the following Control Number: 2001006527

ISBN 978-0-14-250054-5   10 9 8 7 6 5 4 3

The Clubhouse

story by Anastasia Suen
illustrated by Allan Eitzen
based on the characters created by Ezra Jack Keats

Penguin Young Readers
An Imprint of Penguin Group (USA) Inc.

The We
* Certified, cari
* Pre-school th
* Small class siz
* Challenging
* Spanish, art,
AT THE QU
ion C

Peter, Amy, Archie, Lily, and Louie
met at Mrs. Lopez's store.

"Where can we play today?"
asked Peter.

"My baby sister is asleep," said Lily.

"My aunt is visiting," said Archie.

"My mom works at home today,"
said Louie.

"They're painting our apartment,"
said Amy.

"We don't have any place
to play," said Lily.

"We can make a
clubhouse," said Amy.

"A clubhouse?" said Peter.

"Where?"

"Right there," said Lily.

"But how?" said Peter.

"All I see is junk."

"My dad says one man's trash
is another man's treasure," said Louie.

"That's right," said Amy.

"Look over there."

"Wood!" said Lily.

"Let's ask Mrs. Lopez if we can use it!"

Amy and Lily went into the store.
"What a crazy idea," said Peter.
"You can't build a clubhouse with
that junk," Archie said.

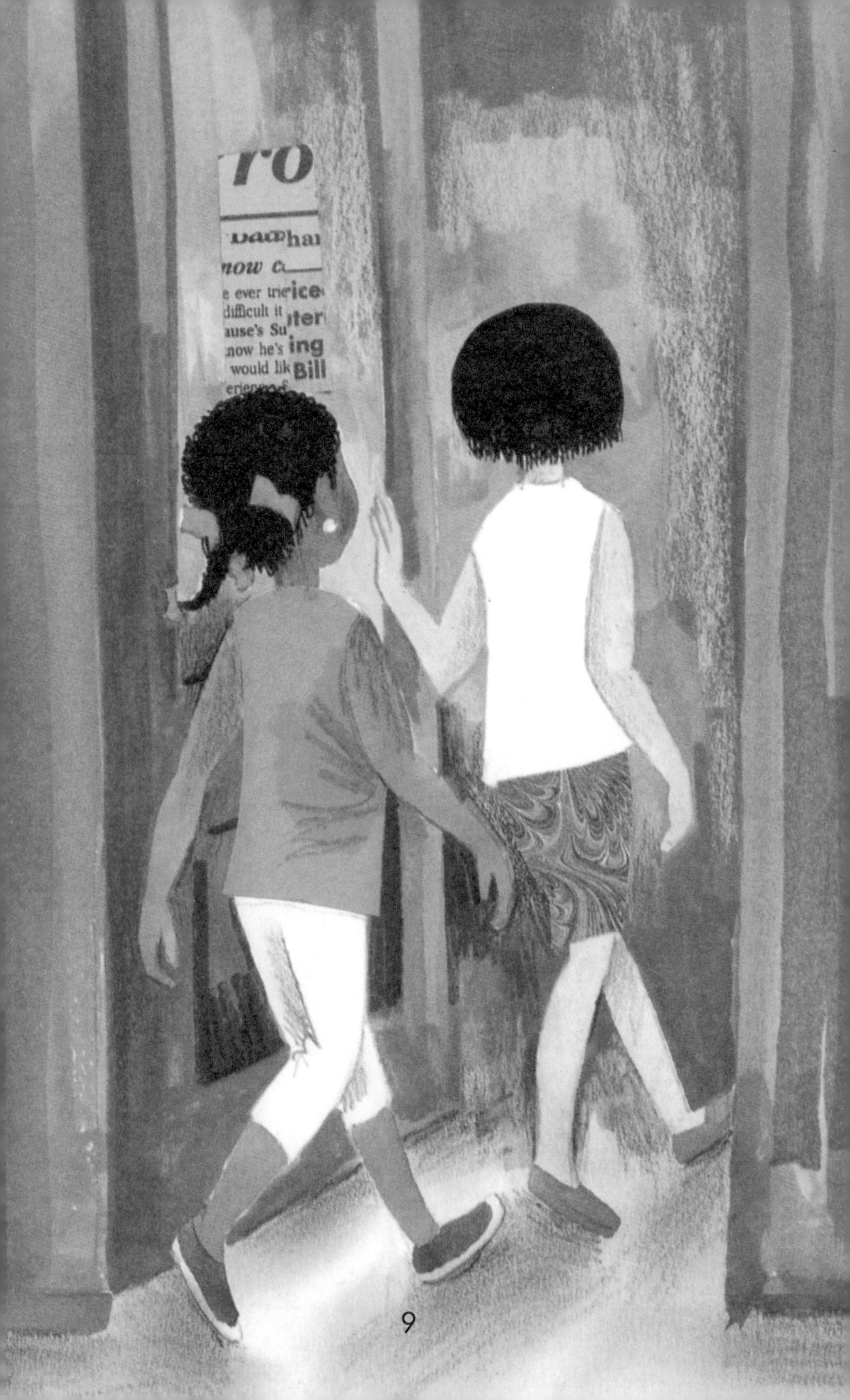

Lily and Amy came out of the store.

"Mrs. Lopez said yes!" said Amy.

"She did?" said Peter.

"Come on," said Amy.

"Okay," said Louie.

And he followed the girls.

"We have to move this trash," said Amy.

She rolled a tire out of the way.

Louie dragged a muffler.

Lily picked up newspapers and boxes.

"There's a lot of trash on that lot,"

said Peter.

"That pipe is in the way," said Archie.

"We can move it," said Peter.

Peter and Archie moved the pipe.

"Now we need wood," said Amy.

Amy pulled on a board.

It was too heavy.

Lily took the other end.

It was still too heavy.

"It looks like they need help," said
Archie.

"You need four people to lift
that one," Peter said.

"We'll help," said Archie.

One, two, three, four!

Up it went!

"Put it here," said Louie.

They put the wood on the ground.

Amy sat on the wood.

"It's perfect," she said.

"It's not a clubhouse yet," said Lily.

"It's not?" said Amy.

"Everyone can see you," said Louie.

"No walls."

"Oh," said Amy.

"Mrs. Lopez said we could use
all the wood," said Lily.

"So let's get busy," said Peter.

They carried all the wood over.

"Now what?" said Amy.

"Hold this board," said Peter.

"I'll hold the other one," said Archie.

"Now put them together," said Lily.

WHAM! The boards fell down.

"We need nails," Peter said.

"Nails?" said Archie.

"Yes, nails," said Lily, and she pointed to Mr. Frank's hardware store.

"Let's go," said Peter.

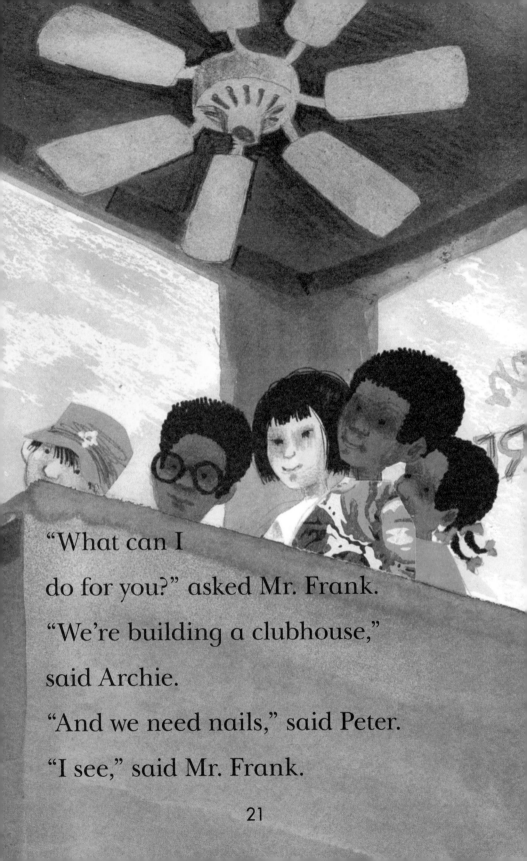

"What can I
do for you?" asked Mr. Frank.
"We're building a clubhouse,"
said Archie.
"And we need nails," said Peter.
"I see," said Mr. Frank.

21

Everyone put money on the counter.

Five nickels, three quarters,

and two dimes.

"You have enough for nails," said

Mr. Frank.

"But you'll need a hammer, too."

"How much is a hammer?" asked Amy.

"Much more than this," said Mr. Frank.

Mr. Frank looked out the window.

"I made a clubhouse

when I was young," he said.

Then he pushed the money away.

"Keep your money," he said.

"You can borrow the hammer and nails."

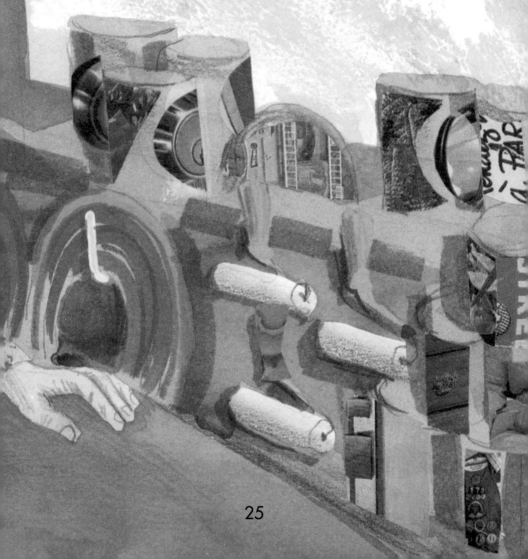

"Thank you, Mr. Frank!" said the kids.

Peter took the hammer.

Amy scooped up the money.

Then they all went back
across the street.

"Here we go," said Lily.

"Hold them tight," said Amy.

Peter hammered in the nails.

BAM! BAM! BAM!

One by one the walls went up.

"Now for the roof," said Louie.

"Here we go," said Peter.

"Lift!"

Peter, Amy, Archie, and Lily
lifted the last board.

BAM! BAM! BAM! BAM! BAM! BAM!

"Wow!" said Louie.

"We did it," said Lily.

"Let's go inside," said Archie.

"It's perfect," said Peter.

"It's not a clubhouse yet," said Amy.

"It's not?" said Peter.

"We need to have a party!" said Amy.

She emptied her pocket.

"Here is our money," Amy said.

"Let's get something to eat."

And so they did.